P9-CAB-558

SEP 2 4 2004
OCT 1 6 2004
NOV 1 1 2004
NOV 2 3 2004
JAN 0 4 2005
JAN 2 6 2005
FEB 2 6 2005
JUL 1 4 2005
OCT 0 1 2005
OCT 1 4 2006
JUL 0 2 2008
JUL 0 7 2008

OCT 1 1 2008
OCT 1 8 2009

Northville District Library
212 W. Cady Street
Northville, MI 48167-1560

COUNTING OUR WAY TO THE
100th Day!

**For my mom,
who likes to do one hundred things at once
—B. F.**

**For my great-grandma Helms,
who lived happily to 101 years old
—S. S.**

Acknowledgments

"All Year Long" and "Estimating Chicken Pox" were first published in
Counting Caterpillars and Other Math Poems (New York: Scholastic, 1998).

"Cass's Coins" was first published in *Poem of the Week, Book 2*
(San Diego: Teaching Resource Center, 1999).

"How We Made 100" was first published in *Write-and-Read
Math Story Books* (New York: Scholastic, 1998).

"My Cousin" was first published in *Poetry Pocket Mini-Books*
(New York: Scholastic, 2001).

Margaret K. McElderry Books
An imprint of Simon & Schuster Children's Publishing Division
1230 Avenue of the Americas, New York, New York 10020
Text copyright © 2004 by Betsy Franco
Illustrations copyright © 2004 by Steven Salerno
All rights reserved, including the right of reproduction
in whole or in part in any form.
Book design by Sonia Chaghatzbanian
The text for this book is set in Barbera.
The illustrations are rendered in gouache.
Manufactured in China
1 2 3 4 5 6 7 8 9 10

Library of Congress Cataloging-in-Publication Data
Franco, Betsy.
Counting our way to the 100th day! /
Betsy Franco ; illustrated by Steven Salerno. p. cm.
ISBN 0-689-84793-9 (hardcover)
1. Schools—Juvenile poetry. 2. Education—Juvenile poetry.
3. Children's poetry, American. 4. Numbers—Juvenile poetry.
I. Title: Counting Our Way to the one hundredth day!.
II. Salerno, Steven. III. Title.
PS3556.R3325 C68 2004
811'.54—dc21
2002153346

FIRST
EDITION

Northville District Library
212 W. Cady Street
Northville, MI 48167-1560

SEP 21 2004

3 9082 09513 6522

COUNTING OUR WAY TO THE 100th Day!

100 poems by betsy franco
with 100 pictures by steven salerno

MARGARET K. McELDERRY BOOKS   New York   London   Toronto   Sydney

Contents

1. On Our Way to the One Hundredth Day

We'll hear 100 first bells ring.
We'll sit in "circle" 100 times.
We'll nibble on 100 snacks.
We'll line up in 100 lines.

We'll sing 100 songs in class.
We'll read 100 books out loud.
We'll bring in our collections, and
we'll all feel very, very proud.

We'll have 100 recesses.
We'll read 100 favorite poems.
We'll come to school 100 times;
100 times we'll go back home.

On each of the hundred days that pass,
we'll always follow the Golden Rule.
That way we'll all be happy when
we reach the *100th Day of School*.

2. Directions for Making 100

Make "100" from the leaves—
in the autumn, when they're bright.

Then arrange 100 snowballs
if the packing is just right.

Plant 100 little seeds
that can drink the springtime showers.

In the summer they'll grow buds,
and you'll have 100 flowers!

3. Things That Can Come in 100

The needles in a little box,
legs on crawly centipedes,
the squares that make a patchwork quilt,
necklaces with little beads,

the trees that fill an orchard up,
the crayons inside a giant pack,
children singing in a choir,
cat's-eye marbles in a sack,

the years that make a century,
stars on two American flags,
the numbers on a hundred grid,
beans inside a small beanbag,

the points on twenty maple leaves,
stamps on great, big, sticky sheets,
and something that is very cool—
days till the 100th Day of School!

4. All Year Long

On a weekend day in springtime,
one hundred boats are on the bay.
Grab your hat, and you can join them
for a wet and wavy day.

In the summer when you're camping,
one hundred lights can fill the sky.
There is nothing quite as special
as a blinking firefly.

When you're walking to the schoolyard
in the brilliant autumn sun,
you may crunch one hundred leaflets,
while you walk or on the run.

On a snowy slope in winter,
you may see one hundred sleds.
You can warm yourself with cocoa
when you finally go to bed.

5.

100 Picnic Pests

55 ants

9 gnats

8 mosquitoes

7 bees

6 spiders

5 slugs

4 crickets

3 fleas

2 flies

1 wasp

Go away,

if you please.

Let us have

our family picnic

underneath

the willow trees.

6. All Our Names

Every person in our class
has something that's the same—
each and every one has got
a cool five-letter name:

Tommy   Reiko

Teddy   Lilly

Kwaku   Ethan

Billy   Sally

Molly   Marco

Amber   Jilly

Pedro   Jonah

Willy   Katie

Nancy   Ralph

Sarah   and Milly!

Count by fives—
they're all the same.
How many letters in
all our names?

7. 100 Cats' Eyes

Two eyes,
       four eyes,
              six eyes bright—
glowing cats' eyes in the night.
Counting's easy in the dark
when each eye's a flashing spark.

As you're counting, use these clues:
Find the pairs and count by twos.
Count beneath the moonlit skies
till you've reached one hundred eyes.

8. one hundred little tiny ants

one hundred

little tiny ants

could fit in the

bowl of a wooden

spoon, but a herd of

one hundred eleph-ants

would take up much,

much, much more

room!

9. Raindrop Races

100 R
      a
         i
            n drops in the rain,
rolling down my windowpane.

R
   a
      c
        i
          n
            g
              running, crashing, splashing,
while the thunderbolts are crashing.

100 r
      a
         i
            n drops in a race,
sliding down
at a very fast pace.

Almost finished, here they come
one by one by one by one.

Hooray! The winning drop is mine!
Here come the other 99
r
  a
     i
       n drops on the windowpane,

having races in the rain!

10. Dandelions

Blow gently on a dandelion
when it's changed its clothes to white,
and then your very special wish
will actually take flight.

One hundred little parachutes
will float around the town
and plant themselves in people's yards
to spread the wishes around.

11. Hey, Look!

Hey, look!
Whatayasay?
I figured out something neat today.
The words "one hundred" have ten letters—
and though it would be much, much better
if they had **100** letters,
there's a way to show one hundred
in an extra-special way:
Write it **10** times in a row.
Just look below!
Now whatayasay?

12. Polka-Dots

I had a little gecko
and her name was "Polka-Dots."

When she was very small,
I counted up her tiny spots.

On her back I counted 78—
on her tail, 22.

When Polka-Dots got bigger,
her spots got bigger too.

13. Quiet and Noisy

If you pat one hundred bunnies,
not a one would make a peep.
But imagine all the "baaa"ing
if you sheared one hundred sheep.

Now, one hundred purple starfish
wouldn't make a single sound,
but one hundred crickets chirping
can be heard for miles around.

If giraffes came by the hundreds,
they would still be very quiet.
But hyenas would be laughing—
that would really be a *riot*!

14. Rainbow Toes

Ten friends
with ten brown toes
run through the sprinkler
in all their clothes.

Ten friends
with ten clean toes
paint them bright
to make them glow.

Ten friends
with rainbow toes
skip around barefoot
wherever they go!

15. Just Wondering

Do 100 dogs fit in a car?
Do 100 rabbits fit in a hat?
Do 100 eggs fit in a shoe?
Do 100 fleas fit on a cat?

Because what if the car was a long limousine?
And what if a magician owned the hat?
And what if the shoe was a giant's shoe?
. . . And never mind about the cat.

17. **Nibble Numbers**

Nibble numbers out of pretzels.
Then sit down and start to eat.
The numbers on the hundred chart
will be your noontime treat.

Ask your friends to come and join you
in your number-nibbling fun.
Don't forget to eat "100"—
it's two zeros and a one!

16. **Billy Crawford-Silver**

Billy Crawford-Silver hasn't
had **100** birthdays yet
or had **100** teachers
or owned **100** pets.

Billy Crawford-Silver hasn't
flown **100** planes
or worked **100** puzzles
or ridden **100** trains.

But Billy Crawford-Silver's
done **100** jumping jacks,
collected **100** baseball cards,
and read **100** paperbacks!

18. **A Size Surprise**

Take a look at the
three biggest coins,
and I'll bet you'll be surprised.
The dollar should be bigger
when you line them up by size.

19. Patchwork Quilt

A quilt can be
one hundred squares.
No matter if they're
hearts or pears
or covered all in
teddy bears.

Just count by tens—
count row by row.
It works to count
both fast and slow.

Ten, twenty, thirty . . .
ready, set, go!

One

Hundred
Unusual
Newts
Dress
Really
Early each
Day.

They meet
at the mucky,
swampy pond,
where they dance
and they sing
and they play.

21. It's Lucky

It's lucky that squirrels
who live in our yards
don't come in one hundred,
or it would be hard.

They'd dig up the grass,
hiding nuts in the fall.
Their spring games of chase
would be wild free-for-alls.

Their nests would be heavy
and branches would break.
What a terrible noise
all their chatter would make.

I'm glad that in my yard
the squirrels come in twos.
'Cause squirrels in the hundreds
would be such bad news.

22. Hide-and-Seek

Playing hide-and-seek—

little Susie's "it."

She counts up to one hundred,

but then she has a fit

'cause everybody hid away

lickety-split,

and then it got to be too late

and everybody

quit!

23. Hats

There once was a boy named Fred
who had **100** hats for his head.
He just couldn't choose
which hat he should use,
so he wore all **100** instead.

24. If "100" Were a Monster

If "100" were a monster,
he would have one hundred eyes,
and "100" would be very old,
but that's not a surprise.

All the children would make glasses
for his hundred googly eyes.
And on Halloween he'd always win
the "scariest-costume" prize.

25. Fish Tanks

100 fish swim in the tanks
we built inside our class.
They splash and dive
and swish their tails,
then turn and kiss the glass.

There are 33 fish in each *zero.*
The *one* has 34.
We clean their tanks and feed them flakes
from the corner grocery store.

26. Potatoes

10 potatoes,
20 potatoes,
30 potatoes,
    and 40.
50 potatoes
60 potatoes
70 potatoes
    look warty.
80 potatoes
90 potatoes
100 potatoes
    in sacks.
Fry them up
on grandma's stove
    and have a yummy snack.

27. Recipe

Take 10 fat purple raisins
and 10 fresh pumpkin seeds.
Add 10 dark chocolate chips
and 10 dried cranberries.

Add 10 banana chips
and 10 sweet cashew nuts,
10 peanuts and 10 walnuts,
and 10 strips from coconuts.

Finish up with 10 brown almonds.
It's a wonderful snack to fix.
Just pour in a bag and shake it.
It's a nutty
    fruity
       sweet and sour
         marvelous
           PARTY MIX!

28. Rest Stop

A spider wove its giant web
before a summer storm.
100 raindrops stopped to rest
until the sun got warm.

29. Laughing

100 ha ha has
100 ho ho hos
100 giggles
100 gasps
100 chortles
100 laughs
Our teacher's counting 100 seconds,
and we are laughing as a class!

30.

SAY THIS POEM FAST OR SLOW
SAY IT FOUR TIMES IN A ROW
IF YOU READ IT THIS WAY
100 WORDS IS WHAT YOU SAY

Clap and snap,
wiggle and hop,
bippity-bippity-bappity-bop.

And when you get
to the very last hop,
please do   not forget to stop.

STOP

31. A Dillar, A Dollar

Four quarters make a dollar.
Twenty nickels, ten thin dimes.
If you have a hundred pennies,
that's a dollar every time.

It would take two half-a-dollars
if you want the same amount,
and, of course, the silver dollar's
worth a dollar when you count!

32. 100 Musical Notes

Pour a cup of one hundred notes
and drink it up with care.
When you open up your mouth,
your songs will fill the air.

Then pour another cup or two
and offer some to me.
Together we can sing a round
or hum in harmony.

33. At the Beach

One hundred clams sleep in the sea.
One hundred bugs climb on the tree.
One hundred crabs crawl on the sand.
How many sand grains on my hand?

34. Which Weighs More?

100 yellow chicks
      or 100 licorice sticks?

100 apple cores
      or 100 wild boars?

100 flapping bats
      or 100 party hats?

100 lemon pies
      or 100 butterflies?

100 caribou
      or 100 of *you*?

35. Bug Parade

20 buzzzzzing bumblebees
go first in the parade.

Then come 20 chameleons
in many different shades.

Behind them 20 serious ants
are marching on the ground,

then 20 gorgeous butterflies
who flutter up and down.

And last come 20 slimy snails
that ooze along the street.

For them to finish the parade
could take about a week.

36. 100 Spots

The baby leopard counted her spots.
She counted in so many ways.
She counted by twos.
She counted by fives.
It took her several days.

She counted her spots by twenties.
She counted them all by tens.
But she always had 100 spots,
though she counted again and again.

37. One Hundred Sparklers

One hundred sweets in a piñata,
one hundred berries fill a pie.
One hundred loaves at Jacob's Deli—
pumpernickel, wheat, and rye.

One hundred fleas can make you itchy,
one hundred gnats can cloud your eyes.
When a pup runs on the beach,
one hundred birds take off and fly.

One hundred tulips burst in springtime,
one hundred sparklers in July.
One hundred wishes make a dreamer,
underneath a starry sky.

38. One hundred watermelon seeds—just spit them out before you eat the watermelon's sweet pink meat.

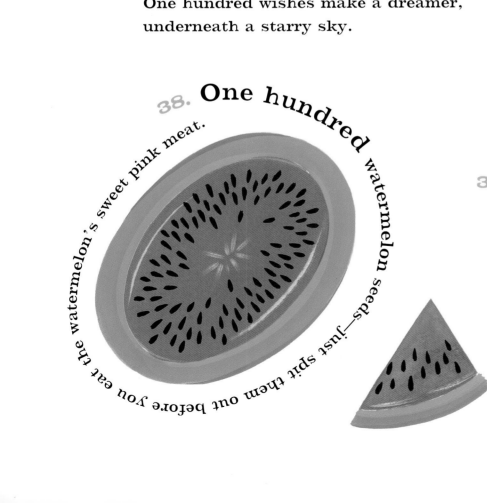

39. 100 Little Letters

With one hundred little letters
you can write a small-sized poem
about pets
or friends
or bumblebees
or rainy days at home!

40. 100 Buzzing Bugs

100 buzzing bugs
making honey in a tree.
If 10 zoom away,
how many would there bee,
buzz-buzz-buzzing in the buckeye tree?

90 buzzing bugs
making honey in a tree.
If 10 zoom away,
how many would there bee,
buzz-buzz-buzzing in the buckeye tree?

80 buzzing bugs . . .

41. 100 Grows

100 kernels
in a pot
are getting
very, very hot.
And when they pop,
then you have got
100 popcorns—
that's a lot.
Putting kernels
in a pot,
100 grows
right on the
spot!

42. Early Morning on the Farm

10, 20   cows to milk

30, 40   eggs in rows

50, 60   sheep to feed

70, 80   plants to grow

90, 100 chores are done.

Hot apple pancakes, everyone!

43. Which Would You Rather Do?

Would you gobble up 100 cakes

or 100 pizza pies?

Would you sleep beside 100 frogs

or 100 butterflies?

Would you choose to bike 100 miles

or climb 100 trees?

Would you rather own 100 snakes

or 100 chimpanzees?

Would you buy 100 baseball caps

or 100 pairs of shoes?

Would you rather feed 100 dogs

or 100 kangaroos?

I know exactly what I'd pick,

but you be the first to choose.

44. Rhyming

I listed the words
that rhyme with "one hundred,"
and all I came up with
is "lightning and thundred."

45. The All-Star Grizzly Band

One hundred grizzlies wait in line
to see the latest show.

Grizzlies gathered for the concert
sit in 20 rows.

Four rows of cool musicians
in the "All-Star Grizzly Band."

Ten bear claws snap the rhythm
on 10 furry grizzly hands.

46. Very Long Animals

We made life-size drawings of animals—
the ones that were big and strong.
Brachiosaurus was 80 feet.
Diplodocus was 90 feet long.

But the one that really outdid them both
was the beautiful, big blue whale.
This creature is 100 feet
from its nose down to its tail!

47. Young and Old

Young

One hundred presents for a newborn,
one hundred days to learn to smile.
One hundred steps is like a journey
to a newly walking child.

Old

One hundred pictures fill her scrapbook—
one hundred laughs for every page.
At her hundredth birthday party
Grams is proud to say her age.

48. Talley's Tallies

Talley tallied one hundred tallies,
with twenty groups in all.
And what was Talley tallying?
The score in basketball!

49. Words Inside "One Hundred"

We made a banner with the words
"One Hundredth School Day."
Then we scrambled up the letters
to make new words to say—
like *noodle, dachshund, horn,* and *tray,*
and *yodel, under, Ron,* and *hay.*
We kept on finding words to make.
We created quite a few.
But we didn't write down all the words—
we left some words for you.

50. Counting Sheep

Tom counts sheep
to go to sleep.
He counts them all by twos.
He tries to count to 100—
that's what he wants to do.
But halfway there,
at 50 sheep,
Tom is usually
fast asleep.

51. Janimals

10 jaguars, 10 jackals,
10 jackrabbits, too.
10 jants, 10 jowls,
10 white jockatoos.
10 jeagles, 10 jolphins,
10 joosters that crow.
10 African jelephants
all lined up in rows!

52. **Under My Bed**

Sometimes I think 100 monsters
live beneath my bed,
and each one has a yellow horn
and a bald and knobby head.

Sometimes when it's a stormy night,
I stand up on the trunk
and ask to join my brother
in the safer upper bunk.

Then he climbs down and checks the room
and tells me it's okay.
And I can close my eyes and sleep
until the break of day.

53. Mystery Animal

I'm known for living one hundred years,
  but I've got lots and lots of fears.
So I hide my head inside my shell
  and tell myself that everything's swell.

Who am I?

54.

My 100th Sandwich

After PB&J for 99 days,
I refuse to eat one more.
Another day of PB&J
would really be a bore.
So I'm keeping just the PB,
and I'm getting rid of the J.
I've got a PB&B with bananas
to eat on the 100th day!

55. Backward

Counting backward from 100
can be tricky, I admit.
But . . .
if you jump right in and start,
I'm sure you'll get the hang of it.

Remember how the astronauts
count back from ten to zero.
Then count the whole way backward,
and you'll be a counting hero!

29

57. **One Hundred Puddles**

One hundred puddles make a pond.
One hundred ponds would make a lake.
One hundred lakes would make a sea.
Just add some salt and sail with me.

One hundred drops can be a cloud.
One hundred clouds can be a storm.
One hundred storms is winter weather.
Let's make a fire and read together.

One hundred words can be a poem.
One hundred poems can be a book.
One hundred books can fill a shelf.
Come read of dragons, bears, and elves.

56. **100 Degrees**

100 below is not
very pleasing
'cause 100 below
is lots colder than freezing.

100 degrees is
a hot summer day.
You can run through the sprinkler
after you play!

58. 100 Is Famous

The number 100 deserves to be famous.
That I can guarantee.
The numbers before it have one or two digits.
100's the first with three!

59. When Beep Got Lost

When my dog, Beep, got lost one night,
I used the computer and started to write.

I made a flyer about his nose,
his fluffy tail, his jet-black toes.

I pasted in a photograph—
the one that always makes me laugh.

I printed out 100 sheets
and rode around 100 streets.

I taped them to 100 poles—
yep, I was really on a roll!

Then someone brought me back my pet.
Hey, that's the happiest I *ever* get!

(I haven't torn down the flyers yet.)

60. I Bet

I bet I could slide 100 times
or lift 100 pounds.
I bet I could jump 100 times
as the jump rope whirled around.

But I bet I could never, ever—
even if I tried—
go back and forth
on the monkey bars
even close to 100 times.

I bet I could eat 100
chocolate-covered lemon drops,
100 pieces of pizza,
or 100 lollipops.

But I bet I could never, ever—
most everyone agrees—
gobble up a little bowlful of
100 black-eyed peas.

61. 100 Inches Tall

If I were 100 inches tall,
I could talk to the birds in the apple tree.
I'd see over everyone in a crowd,
and no one in class would be taller than me.

But . . .
if I were 100 inches tall,
I would bump my head going through the door,
and my bed would be way too short for me,
so I'd have to sleep down on the floor.

I think I'll stay the height I am.
I think I'll stay the same,
except for Saturday afternoons
when I play my basketball games!

62. Ostriches

When Jonah's hundred ostriches
escaped from Jonah's barn,
they ran a hundred miles away
to Old McDonald's farm.

But Jonah found them easily—
that's not what they had planned.
The ostriches had buried their heads
inside a pile of sand!

63. Counting Tricks

1, 2, skip a few, 99, 100.
5, 10, skip again, 95, 100.
10, 20, skipping plenty, 90 and 100.
Now you know some
counting tricks
to skip-count to 100!

64. Counting to the 100th Day of School

Keep count with numbers.
Keep count with stars.
Keep count with beans in a big glass jar.

Keep a long tally
and keep count with pins.
Keep track of how many days there've been.

Keep count by ones.
Keep count by tens.
Keep count each day
and wait, wait, wait.
In February—*C E L E B R A T E !*

65. Families

Six people live
in Becca's house,
including Grampa Lee.

But the mouse living
under Becca's house
has a *hundred*-mouse family.

66. Magnifying Glasses

"100" glasses are easy to make
with colored paper and string.
But when I put my glasses on,
I discover a funny thing.

Things look 100 times bigger
with my "100" glasses on.
An ant is as big as a scorpion;
a wren is as big as a swan.

A bee looks like an airplane,
and my collie, Millicent,
looks just as big, believe it or not,
as a baby elephant!

67.
$100

A hundred dimes would buy a kite.
A hundred pennies buys some gum.
If I had a hundred dollars,
I might buy a kettledrum.

Or I'd treat my friends to pizza,
take them out to movies, too.
If I had a hundred dollars,
I'd have lots of things to choose.

But . . .
if I ever got so lucky that
I had that large amount,
Mom would probably make me
put the money
in a bank account!

68. Buried Treasure

We found some pirate treasure
buried by the maple tree—
50 coins for you,
50 coins for me.
Along came Joey Whitehawk.
Along came Nancy Li.
Now each of us has 25.
We're happy as can be.

69. Paper Loops

We're making 100 loops for a chain.
They're attached like cars on a railroad train.
We each add 5 to the end down there.
It loops under tables and over chairs.
And when we start it at the door,
it goes across the classroom floor!

70. Fancy Shmancy Stamps

Whenever we're out of postage stamps,
  we ask for the newest kind—
    with beetles and flowers,
    musicians and wolves,
    and whatever else we can find.

My mother likes to buy her stamps
  in a big, flat, peelable sheet.
But I think the stamps
all curled like snakes
  are the ones that can't be beat.

71. Sidewalk Squares

The sidewalk squares
are always there.
We walk on them,
but they don't care.

One day I counted
sidewalk squares
to see how many
squares were there.

And when I'd walked
one hundred squares,
I'd hardly traveled
anywhere.

I'd have to walk for hundreds
of squares—for hundreds
    and hundreds
      and hundreds
        of squares—
if I really wanted to get
somewhere.

One Hundred Years

About one hundred years ago
they had just invented the car.
There weren't any TV sets to watch,
and, of course, there were no VCRs.

But in a hundred years from now
a robot'll keep my bedroom clean,
and kids will travel to school each day
by turning on a computer screen.

73. One Hundred's My Favorite Number

It's 25 plus 75
or 97 plus 3.
It's 10 more than 90.
It's the first big number you see!
It's less than 125.
It's 80 dollars and 20 more.
It's the number after 99,
and 104 minus 4!

74. Baby Spiders

Baby spiders come in hundreds,
hatching out of tiny eggs.
What if mama had to teach them
how to use their spindly legs?

Lucky for the mama spider,
newborn spiders spin and walk,
and she needn't teach them words,
for spiders have no need to talk.

75. Moo, Zoo, Loopty-Loo

100 looks like it should rhyme
with words like
zoo and *moo*.
100 looks like it should rhyme
with *boo* and *loopty-loo*.
100 looks like it should rhyme
with words with double Ohs.
But 100 is a number—
it has double ZER-Os!

76. How We Made 100
Poem for Two Voices

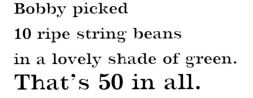

Benny brought in
10 red bugs
in an empty water jug.
That's **10** in all.

Sally brought
10 garter snakes.
Teacher said, "For goodness' sakes!"
That's **20** in all.

Len collected
10 green leaves
from the pretty maple trees.
That's **30** in all.

Cassy wheeled in
10 white cakes
that her Grandma Jenny bakes.
That's **40** in all.

Bobby picked
10 ripe string beans
in a lovely shade of green.
That's **50** in all.

Clare collected
10 small clocks.
Tickity-tock, tickity-tock.
That's **60** in all.

Sammy's got
10 pumpkin seeds,
He can plant them once he weeds.
That's **70** in all.

Ronny has
10 granite rocks
in a little yellow sock.
That's **80** in all.

Talley wore
10 fake tattoos.
Counting can be fun to do.
That's **90** in all.

Me? I blew
10 soapy balls.
That's **100** things in all!

77. A Hundred Pounds

A hundred-pound bird is
   a very large bird,
and a hundred-pound bear
   is a cub.
A hundred-pound pumpkin
   would win at the fair,
and a sandwich
   that heavy's a "sub."

78. Day One Hundred and One

On the 100th Day,
we'll have so much fun.
I feel sorry for day
one hundred and one.

79. Haiku

One hundred acorns
buried all over the yard—
squirrel's autumn chores.

One hundred snowflakes
on my new purple mittens,
melting in the sun.

One hundred red ants
carrying a cookie crumb
in a spring parade.

One hundred mussels
clinging to rocks at the beach.
Ouch! Their shells are sharp.

39

80. When I'm 100

When I'm 100 years old someday,
I might be bald or I might be gray.
My face will have wrinkles.
My hands will have crinkles.
I'll visit my very best friends each day.

I'll walk with a cane
because of my knees.
I'll have lots of cool memories

. . . and I'll do whatever
the heck I please!

81. Estimating Chicken Pox

I estimate my chicken pocks
at a hundred pocks or more.
But when I really count them all,
they total sixty-four.

My brother caught my chicken pox,
and he was itching too.
But my very lucky brother got
two pocks and he was through.

82. Centipede

I have so many little feet—
I've never stopped to count.
They say I have one hundred legs.
That's quite a large amount!

I wait until the moon is out
to hunt for things to eat.
An insect here, an earthworm there
can make a tasty treat.

If you should think to count my legs,
I wouldn't even try.
They look just like a rippling wave
as I go inching by.

83. 100 "Naaa"ing Goats

Farmer Susie had a hundred goats,
and each had a four-sided fence.
But they longed to be together,
and their "naaa"ing made her tense.

So she tore down all the fences,
and she made long pens for ten.
The goats all rearranged themselves
while she tried to sleep again.

But the "naaaa"ing woke the sheep from sleep,
and the cows began to moo.
That woke the baby chicks and pigs—
she didn't know what to do.

But now they never "naaa" at night
while Susie sleeps in bed
'cause she made one big, gigantic pen
where they happily butt their heads.

84. My Cousin

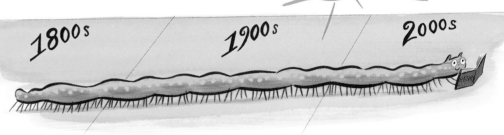

I'm older than my cousin Trix.
When she was five, I was six.
  When Trix is twelve, or twenty-four,
   I'll always be
    just one year more.

   When Trixie's age is ninety-nine,
   just stop and think,
and then guess mine!

85. A Century

A century is a hundred years.
A dollar is a hundred cents.
A meter's a hundred centimeters.
Is all this starting to make some sense?

'Cause "cent" can mean one hundred
in some words that we all know.
Like, a centipede has a hundred legs
that keep him on the go!

86. Great-Grandpa

We pack into the auto
and drive 100 miles.
Great-Grandpa greets us at the door.
His face is full of smiles.
He blows 100 candles out
and one last one for luck.
The table has 100 foods—
it's such a big potluck.
We give him lots of gifts and hugs,
high-fives, and noisy cheers.
He says he can't believe
that he has lived 100 years.
We kiss his happy face
that has at least 100 wrinkles.
Then we drive on back 100 miles
with 100 stars a-twinkle.

87. Balancing

To balance 100 pennies
takes 600 paper clips,
56 cat's-eye marbles,
120 tortilla chips,
36 colorful counting bears,
7 metal cars,
20 pink erasers,
or 6 granola bars!

88. Cass's Coins

Cass collects coins in a cookie jar.
She has a hundred coins so far.
She counts her copper coins with care.
Someday she'll be a millionaire!

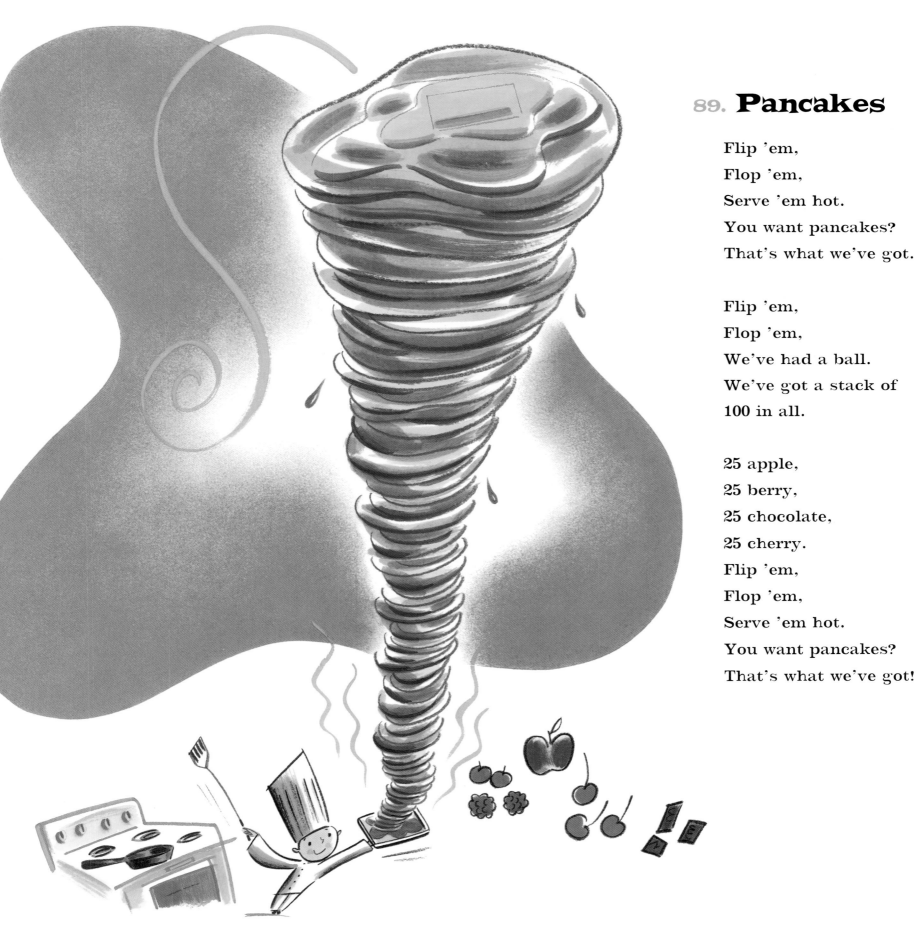

89. Pancakes

Flip 'em,
Flop 'em,
Serve 'em hot.
You want pancakes?
That's what we've got.

Flip 'em,
Flop 'em,
We've had a ball.
We've got a stack of
100 in all.

25 apple,
25 berry,
25 chocolate,
25 cherry.
Flip 'em,
Flop 'em,
Serve 'em hot.
You want pancakes?
That's what we've got!

90. Snowflakes

Little snowflakes—1-2-3
    floating down
    to land on me.

Soon 100 snowflakes swirl
    in a windblown,
    sparkling whirl.

Snowflakes dance before my eyes,
    each a hexagon
    surprise.

Silent and soft in the fading sun.
    They coat the earth
    when the day is done.

91. Schools of Fish, etc.

You'll never see 100 bears
keeping company,
but 100 ants in an army of ants,
or 100 fish in a school of fish,
or 100 toads in a knot of toads,
or a swarm of 100 bumblebees
would be perfectly possible to see.

92. Pictures from "100"

Jimmy made a rocket ship.
Jenny made a cat.
Lily made two baseballs
beside a baseball bat.

Yoko made an alien
with silly, bugged-out eyes.
Terry made an ice-cream cone.
She drew it supersize.

We turned the paper upside down.
We turned the paper round.
We all had so much fun,
we couldn't put our pencils down.

93. Monarch Butterflies

In wintertime there's a certain place
where the monarchs like to be.
They migrate to it every year—
one hundred to a tree.

All folded up, the butterflies
look just like crumpled leaves,
but then they stretch their orange wings
and flutter in the breeze.

94. Snowball Fight

You can make 100
by yourself,
or get your friends to help.
When it's time to throw the snowballs,
you can scream and run and yelp.

When you've tossed 100 snowballs
and you really have no more,
just make another hundred—
because that's what snow is for!

95. High-Five Banner

Our class has 20 kids in it.
We each decide which hand to use
and which of the colors we will pick,
from reds, greens, yellows, oranges, and blues.

We dip five fingers in the paint
and each kid prints a bright "high-five."
5, 10, 15, 20—
all the way to 95.

One more print to
make a hundred.
Kate was late, but
now she's here—
makes a print in
pumpkin orange,
and then we scream
and clap and cheer!

96. 100 Hearts

Kimmy stuck 100 hearts in a specially shaped design. When she was finished, she had made a giant Valentine!

97. Collections of 100

Jill brought nails in rows of ten.
Joey collected 100 cans.
Tim has a chain of paper clips.
Jenny folded 100 fans.

Trisha picked 100 peas.
Ingrid tied 100 bows.
And me? I've got at least 100
freckles on my cheeks and nose!

98. 100 B-Day E-mails

When I opened my birthday e-mails,
you'll never guess what I found—
100 different messages,
and nine of them made sounds!

One from my aunt in Michigan,
six from my very best friend,
one from each of the kids in my class,
and my grandma sent me ten!

Lots from cousins and relatives
and one from a friend in Japan.
A silly pal sent 45—
they were all the same. Go, Ann!

It took me an hour to read them all.
I know 'cause I kept track.
100 e-mails are fun to get
but too many to answer back!

99. Chinese New Year

Chinese New Year
is here again.
We all line up
in groups of ten.
We put on the dragon skins
we made
and dance in
the Chinese New Year's parade!

The Hundredth Day of School!

Our class is just nuts about counting.
We count all the things at our school.
We count in the morning.
We count after lunch.
We all think that counting is cool.

There were 52 kids on the playground.
20 coats in the Lost-and-Found,
16 bikes in a row at the bike rack,
19 backpacks lying around.

Our favorite was counting the school days—
rainy or snowy or gray.
We counted each one as it came and it went,
and now it's the *one hundredth day*!

Let's yell out a **Hip,**

hip,

Hooraaay!

Let's shout even louder

Hooraaay!!!!!